Coffee Talk 2

An Uncle and His Nephew
Discuss Faith and Science

By

J.R. Dickens

This story is a work of fiction, but it sure has a lot of truth in it. Any resemblance between the author and the character named "Uncle Bob" is probably coincidental—although it's true the author's middle name is *Robert* and he has been an uncle since the age of eight.

ISBN (Print Edition): 978-0-9992870-1-9

Introduction

This book is the second installment in the *Coffee Talk* series and follows up on the previous discussion between Uncle Bob and his nephew on the nature of truth.

Like the first volume, this book was written as an in-depth conversation that allows our characters to delve into some important questions—in this case, the philosophical aspects of faith and science. It's a quick read but is worthy of study in order to get the most out of it. Refer to the back of the book and you'll find a number of review questions as well as a Glossary to help you navigate the terminology. Glossary terms will be shown in **boldface** the first time they're introduced.

My intent with this series is to raise the

level of discourse regarding matters of ultimate importance. We urgently need to learn how we can connect more meaningfully, think more carefully, and converse more respectfully. Toward that end, I hope this book will be a blessing to you.

Pour yourself a cup of coffee and join in the conversation.

J.R. Dickens

Woodland Park, Colorado

Chapter 1

It's bright and early on a Saturday morning in your quiet neighborhood when the coffee maker springs to life with the click of a switch. The first noise is a slight sizzle from the burner as it begins to heat the soggy bottom of the coffee pot. Moments later, the first gurgles emanate from inside the reservoir as hot water begins to make its way through the coffee grounds and trickle down into the pot. Drip, drip, drip. The pleasant aroma of brewing coffee begins to fill the kitchen. Within a few minutes, the last of the hot water is draining into the filter basket and the black brew is now standing by for duty.

Two clean mugs already sit on the counter—one for you, and one for Uncle Bob. He's on his way over to your house to share some morning Joe and good conversation. You've been thinking about this meeting for several days and looking forward to discussing some things that have been bothering you after reading a series of scientific articles in the local newspaper. The author of the articles— a science & technology reporter—has a way of speaking that makes everything about science sound utterly convincing. But despite the reporter's certitude, you find yourself wrestling with nagging doubts about some of the statements he makes in his articles. Something seems a little off. Maybe Uncle can help clear up the confusion.

A few weeks earlier, you enjoyed a long conversation with Uncle Bob following an impromptu encounter with several neighbors that left you pondering the nature of truth. In the course of a morning stroll, you'd discovered firsthand how there is a bewildering assortment of conflicting opinions about something that you'd always taken for granted. Uncle then took you on a challenging journey across the landscape of philosophy in order to help you understand that the existence of truth is foundational to all kinds of knowledge—including scientific knowledge. But as you realized at the time, there was a great deal more to say on the topic of science.

A rap on the front door brings your thoughts back to the present. Uncle is here!

Chapter 2

After briefly taking in your disheveled appearance, Uncle steps over the threshold and offers a timid smile. "I hope I'm not here too early. From your message last night you sounded eager to talk."

You self-consciously suppress a yawn and reply, "I've been up for a while." (Okay, not really.) "Thanks for coming over."

"Do I smell coffee?"

"Yes. Please help yourself. Everything is on the counter. I'll join you in a few minutes." As you make your way to the bathroom, Uncle steps into the kitchen to pour a cup. You were hoping for just enough time to improve your appearance before Uncle arrived, but he thwarted your plan by arriving early, as is his habit.

By the time you make it back to the kitchen, Uncle is halfway through a cup of coffee and has set out some toast and jelly.

"I took the liberty of making a quick breakfast to go with the coffee. Nothing fancy."

Uncle was being kind. There was nothing fancy in your kitchen to prepare.

He tries to make a bit of conversation as your mental engine continues to warm up. "Is this a new brand of coffee you're using? It has a nice smooth flavor."

How Uncle could tell the coffee had changed was a mystery. His beverage never even resembled coffee by the time he'd added generous helpings of cream and sugar. Latte, maybe, if that still qualifies as coffee.

"Uh, yeah. *Maryland Club* if I recall. I honestly wasn't paying much attention to the brand when I picked it up this week. It was on sale."

After pouring your own coffee you take a seat at the table and reach for the toast.

Uncle butters a slice of toast and adds some jelly. "I suppose you've had quite a bit to think about since our last conversation. What were the big takeaways for you?" Uncle is hoping his question will help you get your mind in gear. It could be another challenging day.

After a moment of thought, you wash down a bite of toast with coffee and try to summarize the big idea from your previous conversation. "I honestly don't remember all the new terms you used, but it boils down to the fact that conflicting ideas can't all be right." You can feel the coffee gradually beginning to work its magic.

"Good. What else?"

"Well, you had a lot to say about science

during our discussion of philosophy. That's what is mainly on my mind today."

"And what did we discuss about science that is giving you some lingering concerns?"

"You said something about scientists having to rely on faith. I guess I still don't see what faith has to do with science."

"Of course. The connection isn't obvious at first. We are used to thinking about science in concrete terms because of what it *does*, not in abstract terms because of the **presuppositions** it relies on."

Ouch. It's way too early in the morning for Uncle to start unleashing the big words. He senses your discomfort.

"Remember how we talked last time about **axioms**? Those are things you have to *presuppose* because they can never be proved. Everybody has axioms—absolutely everybody. But we easily take them for granted and oftentimes have no idea we're even using them."

You're now beginning to remember a bit more from the previous conversation. "And that's what you meant when you said that scientists have to have faith." Stated as a half-question to hedge your bets.

"Exactly. Axioms form the basis for scientific inquiry. We'll unpack that idea some more today. But also remember we talked about another aspect of scientific faith: assumptions regarding things like the origin of the universe that are often presented as 'facts' even though they are scientifically unfalsifiable."

Oh boy. The conversation is revving up faster than your mind.

Chapter 3

Uncle is already starting to get lost in his own thoughts. "Science works in three basic ways. One—**observation**. Just looking at what's happening around us right now. Watching the grass grow or watching a bird build a nest. Two—**experimentation**. Setting up a test in a controlled environment in a way that makes it possible to answer a certain question."

"You mean the **hypothesis**?"

"Yes. Specifically, a question that can be *disproved* by the experiment. And three—**forensics**. Examining historical evidence in order to discover something about the past."

"Like *CSI?*"

"Yes, very much like the work of a crime scene investigator. But forensic science is the weakest of the three approaches, for reasons we'll see later."

Maybe the coffee is working better than you thought. "But don't some scientists just work in the realm of **theory**?"

"Good question. Yes, we may develop complex theories on paper. But it's normally with the intent of making observations or running experiments that will support or contradict the theory."

"Do you mean that the theory tells us how something is *supposed* to work?"

"You might say that the 'cash value' of a theory is how accurately it makes predictions. For example, there was considerable controversy at the beginning of the 20th century regarding Einstein's theory of **relativity**. It required a special kind of observation to determine if Einstein got it right. His theory was that gravity (as from a star) would change the shape of space—to bend it like a window screen might bend when you push against it. So the theory was used to predict how much distortion would occur in the star field surrounding the sun during a total eclipse. The stars closest to the sun would appear to be slightly out of position because of the distorted space around the sun."

Okay, that was way more than you wanted to know. "And Einstein was proved right?"

"In a manner of speaking. But we should be more precise about the way we describe the scientific method."

"How do you mean?"

"Let's use the analogy of a courtroom proceeding to better understand how science works. Are you familiar with the concept of 'innocent until proven guilty'?"

"Sure. It means that if I'm accused of a

crime, the prosecution has to present evidence to prove that I'm guilty."

Uncle is impressed. "Indeed. But what is the alternative to the **presumption of innocence**?"

"Well, I guess we could assume that everyone is guilty until proven innocent."

"And which assumption do you suppose is more difficult to overturn?"

Uncle is starting to test you a bit too early in the discussion. "I might need to think about that for a moment."

"No problem. I'll help myself to another cup of coffee and some more toast. Would you like a warm up?"

Without waiting for an answer, Uncle fetches both coffee mugs as he pushes back from the table.

Chapter 4

By the time Uncle sits back down at the table, you think you have an answer to the question. "If I've committed a crime, there would probably be some evidence left behind. Maybe a fingerprint that puts me at the scene. Or an eyewitness. But if we start by presuming that I'm guilty, it doesn't matter whether there's any evidence connecting me to the crime."

"The **burden of proof** would be on *you* to prove your innocence. And what if you couldn't do that?"

"Then I'd be convicted of a crime I didn't commit."

"And that would be a miscarriage of justice." Uncle sees you're on the right track but still need a bit of prompting. "So which presumption is more difficult to disprove?"

"If we presume innocence, it might only take a fingerprint to prove guilt. But if we presume guilt. . . ."

"You'd better have a good attorney and an airtight alibi."

Uncle's point is starting to sink in. "Proving my innocence might be impossible."

"As a practical matter, you couldn't do it. If you failed to present overwhelming evidence—if there was any lingering doubt at all about your *innocence*—you'd still be convicted. Remember that the prosecution would have to prove nothing in order to get a conviction."

"Wow. That's a scary thought."

"Odds are we'd all be in jail for something. But when we presume innocence, the prosecution now carries the burden of proof. If they fail to present adequate evidence—if there are serious doubts about your *guilt*—then you'd be acquitted."

"I'm innocent."

You walked right into Uncle's trap. "Technically, *no*. You are found 'not guilty'—which is to say, that you have not been *proved* guilty. Remember your innocence is a starting assumption."

"And that means I could still be guilty, but the prosecution simply didn't prove the case?"

"That is correct. It happens all the time. And the scientific method operates exactly the same way. Our theories are *presumed* to be true until *proven* false by the evidence. Scientific theories are never proven to be true because such proof would require unlimited knowledge. It's unattainable."

"So there might always be some doubt

about a scientific theory?"

"Correct. And that's why every theory should be continually viewed with a degree of skepticism."

"Because theories can be disproved from just one experiment?"

"Or one observation."

"But doesn't that mean that we could be wrong and not know it?"

"Yes. Even when the data *seems* to line up with the theory, we could still be wrong for a variety of reasons. And we never have *all* the data. That's precisely why the hypothesis should always be stated in a way that makes it easy to falsify."

"Now I remember what you said last time about science discarding its old theories."

"Yes. As we observe more of nature, and as we run more experiments, we reject those theories that no longer explain the data."

"Uncle, if it's the case that our theories are only assumptions until *disproved*. . . ."

"Then we begin to understand more clearly why it is that science must operate on faith."

The implications are sinking in. "That's alarming."

Uncle nods. "That's just the tip of the iceberg."

Chapter 5

"Before we look more closely at the necessity of faith, I want to tie up a loose end from our discussion about innocence and guilt. You saw how, in the courtroom analogy, it was possible for two kinds of mistakes to occur."

"With the **presumption of guilt**, I could easily be convicted of a crime I didn't commit."

"And what else?"

"With the presumption of innocence, I could be declared 'not guilty' when I actually committed the crime."

"Exactly. The same types of errors are possible in many kinds of decision-making processes. In science, we propose a theory that is actually wrong, but as yet we don't have enough evidence to discard it. We call this 'failure to reject' a **Type 1 Error**. Or, we could mistakenly throw away a theory when it's actually true. This is called a **Type 2 Error**."

The labels strike you as clunky, but maybe it still helps to put a name on them. "What can we do to keep from making these kinds of errors?"

Uncle sighs. "We can't eliminate them. We can only trade them off. In other words, the more we try to reduce one, the more we make of the other. Let me use an industrial example to illustrate the problem."

Uncle takes a long slurp of coffee and stares at the cup as he places it back on the table.

"In the world of quality control, we work very hard to eliminate defects from the manufacturing process. The goal is to make sure the customer never buys an item with a defect. Sounds like a simple problem, but it's actually quite difficult to do."

"Why not just find everything with a defect?"

Uncle looks up from the cup. "That's precisely the problem. Let's say the customer has been complaining about receiving defects—at the rate of 5%, for the sake of argument. One in twenty items has something wrong with it. So we tighten our inspection process to catch that pesky 5% before it goes out the door. But there's another side to the equation that the customer doesn't see. It's everything good we have to reject."

"What do you mean? Why would you reject something that isn't defective?"

"Because the more carefully we inspect, the harder it becomes for us to tell the good items from the bad ones. So when we tighten the inspection process to make sure we catch all the *bad* ones. . . ."

"Then we end up rejecting more of the good ones."

"And that's the dilemma. We want to eliminate the Type 1 Error—*missed defects*—but the more we reduce this error risk, the more Type 2 Errors we make—*false calls*. Rejecting good items. And as you might imagine, there's a cost to rejecting a good item."

You think you're following Uncle's train of thought back to the courtroom. "So we presume innocence to minimize the risk of convicting an innocent person, but we trade that for a higher risk of acquitting the guilty."

"Yes, that's how the system is designed to work. If we presumed guilt, the results would be reversed."

"More innocent people convicted, and fewer guilty that go free. But we still make both kinds of errors."

"It is literally impossible to drive the risk of a Type 1 Error to zero—and in the meantime, the risk of a Type 2 Error skyrockets. This is an important concept, so let me give you another illustration of the problem." Uncle empties the cup and returns it to the table. "In the world of healthcare, there is a big push for more screening examinations. The idea is that if you have a serious disease like cancer, your odds of effective treatment improve with early detection. And since our screening technology has improved drastically, early detection is more feasible."

"That's all good, isn't it?"

"Not necessarily, because the harder we look at the human body, the more likely we are to find 'abnormalities'—something that isn't quite right. Now the dilemma with early detection is that we are able to find more *ab-normalities*, but we have no way of knowing whether they require treatment. By looking more closely and more frequently at the human body, we do indeed catch a little more of the disease. . . ."

"But we also catch a lot of stuff that isn't really a problem."

"And because we can't tell the benign abnormalities from those that pose a danger to the patient, we end up treating otherwise healthy people for things that would never have bothered them."

"So a few people benefit from screening, but many more are over-treated?"

"Yes. And that's the way Type 1 and Type 2 Errors always work. We don't want to miss a real incidence of disease, but the harder we try to eliminate a *missed* diagnosis, the more likely we are to make a *false* diagnosis. And it doesn't take a lot of imagination to see how that second error imposes a high cost to the system. We wrongly assume we can eliminate the *missed* diagnosis—which is the Type 1 Error—and we ignore the rapidly escalating cost of *over*-diagnosis—which is the Type 2 Error. And the Type 2 Error is insidious precisely because we wrongly assume we're treating more disease."

Once again you find yourself feeling uncomfortable. Maybe science isn't quite as scientific as you've been led to believe. "Where do we draw the line?"

"That's the million-dollar question: when is the 'abnormal' *normal?* And we don't know how to answer it. In fact, simply asking the question opens a can of worms." Uncle shakes his head as if he's stopping himself from getting sidetracked. "Now let's bring that idea back to the question of scientific theories so we can see how science works. But first, a quick break."

Uncle pushes back from the table and helps you clear away the remainder of the breakfast items.

Chapter 6

A fresh pot of coffee is now brewing, but the kitchen is otherwise quiet. Uncle knows you need some time to process everything you've heard this morning. He has just finished rinsing the dishes from breakfast while you were putting the butter & jelly back into the refrigerator.

Uncle now breaks the silence. "Why don't we sit on the patio for a while since it's a nice morning?"

With fresh coffee in hand, the two of you step out onto the patio and ease into the cushions of the reclining chairs. It's a warm morning with a gentle breeze. Sunlight dances in the shadow of the leaves as it filters through the tall trees. A waning crescent moon hangs like a pale ornament over the western horizon.

"Let's think about how science works by taking an absurd example. An astronomer looks at the moon through his telescope and proposes a theory that it's made out of green cheese. He doesn't know, of course. But the theory is supported to some extent by observation—the moon *looks* a little like green cheese—and more importantly, the theory gives him a starting point for further investigation."

"The point of science isn't to stop once there's a theory." Another half-question.

"As you surmise, a theory is just a convenient starting point. It's like an arrow that points us along a certain line of investigation when we don't know which way to go. What might come next?"

"Collect evidence . . . to *disprove* the theory."

"So we make a quick trip to the moon, bring back a rock, and after some laboratory analysis, we determine that the composition of the rock is minerals and metals. No sign of cultured dairy products."

"We've disproved the theory."

"And we did it with one rock. But couldn't we still be wrong?"

"Well, I suppose." You take a moment to think about the question before continuing. "Maybe we just happened to pick up the only rock that *isn't* made of green cheese."

Uncle laughs out loud. "Good insight! So how did we use the rock—a single data point, as it were—to disprove our original theory?"

You come to a sudden halt. "I'm not sure I follow."

"In the world of science we have to rely heavily on a rational process called **induction**. It's how we extrapolate a little bit of data in an effort to explain something much bigger. So when we pick up *one* moon rock and find that it's made of minerals and metals. . . ."

You finish Uncle's thought. "Then we conclude *all* the rocks on the moon are made of minerals and metals."

"And we have to make that kind of a leap because. . . ?"

"Well, because we could never collect and test *all* the rocks on the moon."

"So notice how, on the basis of one rock, we rejected our old theory and replaced it with a new and hopefully better one: *the moon is made of minerals and metals*. And we used induction to formulate the new theory."

Suddenly you begin to see that induction really is quite a leap. "So would you say that induction is the way we fill the gaps in the data?"

"Remember that science operates mostly in the dark—with just a small amount of data. That's why we formulate theories that are easy to falsify, and it's also why we rely on induction to make inferences."

"So with our new theory in hand, we now collect more rocks."

"And guess what—it's an expensive proposition. But let's say we go back to the moon and bring back a hundred rocks this time. And sure enough, every one of them has the same basic mineral-metal composition as the first rock we examined. Have we proved our new theory?"

"Of course. All the data agrees."

"Hmm, not so fast. A hundred rocks is a decent start, but how much of the moon is still unexplored?"

You feel slightly rebuked. "Well, most of it. In fact, almost all of it."

"In comparison to the size and volume of the moon, even a hundred rocks is less than a speck of dust. And notice we've only collected what's easy to collect—rocks sitting on the surface."

"So maybe the whole interior of the moon is made of green cheese, but we haven't even started to explore it yet."

Uncle grins. "You're beginning to understand the challenge of science—what it can do and what it can't do. How it must operate on a host of assumptions. How data moves the needle so that we can improve our assumptions over time."

"But we can never know enough to 'prove' our theories."

Uncle takes a long sip of coffee as if to savor your moment of insight. He is now preparing to unfold the next part of the lesson.

Chapter 7

"The moon problem points out how we must rely on small samples of data in order to test our theories and make inferences. The way we collect samples is critical, because it's the only data we'll have to work with. But **sampling** is almost invariably biased in some way. Often for very practical reasons."

You ponder Uncle's statement. "If we want more moon rocks, we'll be limited in terms of how many we can collect, how big they are, and where we pick them up. It would be too costly to take samples from the whole surface, or to take deep core samples that would reveal the composition on the interior."

"Quite observant. So we often rely on samples that are easy to collect and small in number because of the cost or time involved.

Now, what is the danger of this kind of non-random sampling?"

You're momentarily sidetracked by the new term. "Well, I could say there is no danger—but only if. . . ."

"Go on."

"Only if the moon were perfectly uniform. Then it wouldn't really matter which rocks we picked up, or how many. They would all tell us exactly the same thing."

"Yes, very good! But as we've already seen, it's possible we're wrong about the moon being the same on the inside as it is on the outside. Natural variation is part of what makes inference a dangerous game. There could be a lot of green cheese hidden under the rocks and dust on the surface."

Uncle takes a sip of coffee before finishing his thought. "And that's why we continue to collect more data and compare it to our expectations. When the data no longer fit properly, we know it's time to start looking for a new theory."

"So a theory doesn't have to be correct to be useful. What if every theory turns out to be wrong?"

"The nature of theories is that we formulate them on the basis of just a little information, and we try to formulate them in a way that explains as much of the data as easily as possible. But the odds are that some parts of the data aren't explained by the theory."

"I'm struggling to follow. Can you put this in simpler terms?"

"Hang on." Uncle leaps from the chair and disappears into the house. A few minutes later he is back on the patio with a pen and a writing pad. He scribbles for a moment and then shows you his hasty artwork:

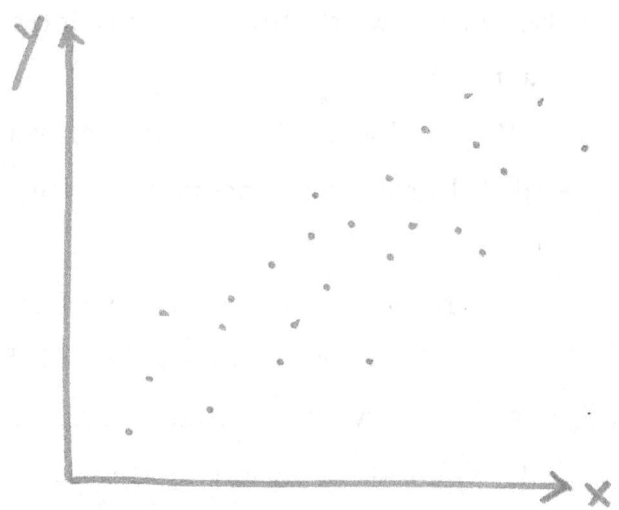

"Let's say we take some measurements of y in relation to x and plot them on a graph like so. What do you see?"

"I see what looks like a relationship. As x goes up, y goes up."

"Yes, there's clearly an association of some kind. We call it a **correlation**. Now, what would be the easiest way to show how x and y behave in relation to each other?"

"We could draw a line through the data. But it wouldn't fit the data perfectly."

"Quite right." Uncle adds a line over the data and shows you the result.

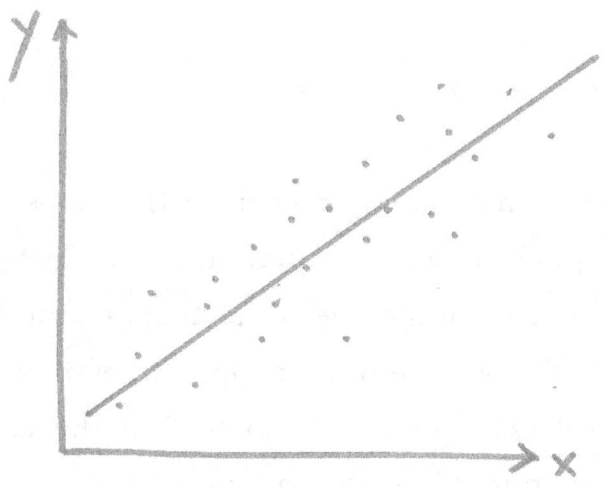

"The simplest relationship between x and y is a straight line. In this case, it looks like the line explains about 80% of the relationship between x and y."

"And what about the rest?"

"Some of it must be noise, but we don't know how much. Clearly something else is affecting the relationship between x and y, but we can already explain most of it with a simple line." Uncle adds the equation for a line to his graph:

$$y = mx + b$$

You immediately recognize the slope-intercept form of the equation from algebra. "You're saying the line is the 'theory' that describes how x and y behave in relation to each other. We just need to find the constants m and b in the equation."

"Yes, very good. We call this a *model*. It's not perfect, but it gives us a good starting point."

"So in one respect, the model—the line—is wrong because it doesn't fit all the data.

But since it explains *most* of the relationship, it's useful?"

"What you just said is almost an exact quote from a famous statistician. He said, 'All models are wrong. Some are useful.' So, how might this model be useful to us?"

"Well, you just showed that the model gives us a simple way to explain the existing data."

"And what else might we want to do with the model?"

The question sinks in. "Well, I suppose we could use the model to help fill in the gaps."

"Yes, a useful model is one that we can use to *predict*. And that brings us to another idea that we easily take for granted."

"You mean, that we can predict something before it happens? Like the weather?"

"Yes, and what would have to be true in order for us to make any prediction of future events? What axiom is required?"

You aren't quite prepared for that question. Uncle knows it's a stretch, but he likes to see how far he can push you. "I don't think I'm following you."

"It's okay. I don't expect you to know the terminology, but you'll easily understand the concept. It's called **uniformity** and it means that the universe operates in a predictable manner. What we observe in the *past* can be used to predict the *future*. It means that the relationships between variables like x and y are consistent from time to time and place to place."

"Uncle, that seems obvious, but you say it as if we don't have a good reason to believe it."

"Without a doubt, we take uniformity for granted. The question is whether we have a good *reason* for doing so. Do you remember how we talked last time about the idea of a self-created universe? A universe governed—so to speak—by pure chance?"

"Yes, now that you mention it, the discussion is coming back to me."

"Good. So the question is, why should we expect a random, self-created universe—if that's really what it is—to consistently behave as if there were some fixed laws of nature?"

You feel yourself beginning to perspire slightly even though the patio is actually quite comfortable with the cool morning breeze.

Chapter 8

Your head is still spinning when Uncle continues the discourse.

"Without the axioms of induction and uniformity, science would be in big trouble. *Induction* allows us to make broad generalizations from just a little data, and *uniformity* makes it possible for us to predict the future from the past. Take away either assumption, and science is dead as a doornail. No matter how much data we collect, we'd have no way to make sense of it. The data would be useless."

Uncle pauses briefly before whacking the next extra-base hit—an opposite-field triple into the right field corner. "And as we discussed last time, science relies on axioms like logic and math. But it also relies on

sense perception."

You're beginning to feel like you're headed back down a bottomless pit and you'll never understand all the ideas Uncle is throwing at you. But you take some comfort in the certainty that he *wants* you to understand and won't let you slip into a free fall.

Uncle slows the pace slightly. "Last time we discussed the importance of **epistemology**—the science of knowledge. How we know what we know. We saw how the relativist is in a bind because he denies the existence of objective reality. He would say there is nothing out there to know. If he's right, science is a moot point because there's nothing to discover. And the other problem for the relativist is that he can't trust his own senses. Whatever he *thinks* he sees or hears or touches or tastes or smells is just the product of his imagination."

You now see where Uncle is going. "The scientist can't do science unless he can trust his own senses to discover something about objective reality."

"Excellent! And I hope you see that it's necessary to assume your senses are reliable because you can't prove it. Let's put it this way to make the point: Your senses are the only contact you have with the world outside of your own mind, and you therefore must trust that your perception of reality is accurate."

Uncle's statement triggers a movie memory. You blurt out, "Otherwise we're like Neo trapped in the Matrix—permanently immersed in a tub of pink goo but convinced that we're living a real life in a real city."

"Yes, I suppose that's one way of looking at it. Hypothetically, if you could apply the proper electrical stimulation directly to the

47

brain, it would be impossible for someone to know the difference between a dream and reality. All sense perception, ultimately, is just electrical activity interpreted by the brain."

At that very moment, you notice three neighborhood kids as they pedal down the street on their bikes. They're weaving erratically, narrowly avoiding each other as they jockey for position. Uncle uses the opportunity to explain what you're already wondering.

"I can hear the wheels grinding. Let me guess. You want to know how it is that we take so much for granted." Sometimes you wonder whether Uncle is telepathic. He's not, but he is clever enough to steer you along with the conversation. He can do that because he's already been down the path.

You begin to speak as the thought is falling together in your mind. "Those kids on their bikes don't know any of this stuff. But they already take it for granted, don't they?"

"How else could you do something as complex as riding a bike? Of course. From a very young age we internalize these kinds of assumptions, and most of us are never challenged to question them."

"So you'd even say that it takes a lot of faith just to ride a bike."

Uncle watches the young bikers sail precariously around the corner and disappear from view. "More than you may know."

This has been a long morning, but you're already beginning to understand more clearly why you were bothered by the science articles in the newspaper. There was an unmistakable air of certainty—maybe even smugness—that seemed unwarranted by the complexity of the topic. If science really has to rely so much on *faith*, perhaps it should make an effort to project a bit more humility.

Chapter 9

Since discovering your Uncle's fondness for ham and cheese sandwiches during his previous visit, you're more than adequately prepared for lunch this time around—even down to his favorite brands of wheat bread and cheddar cheese.

The lunch break comes at a good time. Uncle is gracious enough to make small talk while your brain recovers from the intense morning workout. "I spoke to your dad earlier this week. He says you're settling into your new neighborhood and feeling more comfortable at work." Uncle takes a ravenous bite of ham and cheese as if he hasn't eaten in a week.

As you recall, Uncle is five years older than your dad, who lives in another part of the country with your mom. Your two younger sisters are still in college, so mom and dad are empty nesters unless one of the kids return home to the roost after graduation.

"It's a friendly neighborhood, and I enjoy the work," you say, somewhat vacantly. "But it's been hard moving so far away from where I grew up."

"You're going through one of the hardest transitions in life," Uncle offers. He knows there are harder ones yet to come.

"The workplace is starting to feel like my new family. That's not surprising since we spend so much time together. But it's been a steep learning curve, too. Even when I'm putting in extra hours, I'm having a hard time keeping up."

"You'll find your groove. Meantime, use the opportunity to learn everything you can."

Uncle takes another big bite of ham and cheese and chases it with a handful of kettle chips. The crunch is nearly loud enough to draw complaints from the neighbors.

"College didn't really prepare me for this."

"Of course it didn't," Uncle concludes with a chuckle, as if anyone ought to know that. Followed by more crunching. Uncle seems to be particularly fond of the barbeque-flavored chips.

Chapter 10

After clearing the table, you and Uncle each take a comfortable chair in the living room. The idea of a nap sounds really appealing, but you know that's not going to happen. Class is back in session. You suspect Uncle wishes he had a bell to ring.

"How has the conversation this morning added to your understanding of the scientific enterprise?" Uncle likes to ask questions to reengage the discussion. And he sometimes sounds corny in the process. *Scientific enterprise.*

After some thought, you reply, "I think I'm beginning to understand why science has to rely on so many assumptions in order to discover new knowledge. But even so, it sounds like progress is a painfully slow process."

"And riddled with uncertainties all along the way. Most of them unknowable, except perhaps in hindsight."

"I find myself wondering how scientists can speak in a way that makes them sound so certain of what they think they know."

"You may recall a comment I made the last time we talked. Scientists can be blinded by what they already know. Expertise easily breeds overconfidence. Even the most brilliant scientists are quite susceptible to **groupthink**."

"Is that what you mean when you say scientists are biased?"

"We are *all* biased by what we know—or what we *think* we know. We all see the world through a certain set of lenses. The more certain we are, the harder it is to see things that don't agree with our expectations. No one is ever really neutral."

"Is that why people have such resistance to new ideas?"

"I'm sure that's a big part of it. Expectations shape our understanding of what is possible, so we naturally reject what doesn't seem possible. But there are a number of other reasons why we resist new ideas. We can be deeply and personally invested in a certain idea, so we naturally want to defend it."

"Then how is it that *you* seem to have a knack for seeing things in a different way?"

Uncle chuckles. "With training and practice, we can begin to uncover and examine our own assumptions. But it's still the case that we each maintain an assortment of biases."

"And didn't you say last time that scientists aren't taught to think like philosophers?"

"You could earn a dozen science degrees and never be exposed to the *philosophy* of science. You're like those kids on the bikes— pedaling away in your laboratory, publishing articles and writing books without a second thought about the assumptions you have to make in order to do science."

"Assumptions like uniformity and induction and sense perception."

"Yes, assumptions that literally make it safe to get out of bed in the morning. And while we're at it, let's add another important one to our list of scientific presuppositions: **causality**."

Uh oh. Uncle has stoked the boiler and the train is now leaving the station. *Mind the gap!*

Chapter 11

"Causality—which refers to cause-and-effect—is taken for granted in the world of science but it turns out to be a tricky concept. There's a big difference between observing events occurring in a sequence and being able to attribute causation to the earlier event. As a practical matter, causality can never be proved."

"So it must be assumed like an assortment of other. . ."

"*Presuppositions*. Or axioms. Now take a look at my beautiful graph one more time. We can plainly see that x and y are related—*correlated*, to use the statistical label—but this graph tells us nothing about the nature of the relationship. We could be taking a big risk to suggest that x *causes* y, or vice versa.

It may simply be the case that these two variables move up and down at about the same time."

"So what happens if we attribute causation to x?"

"What do you think?" Uncle is always looking for ways to help you work out your own answers.

"I could be disappointed if I try to control y by changing x."

Uncle laughs. "Probably. It might work and it might not. But you could spend a lot of time adjusting x in a vain attempt to control y. Now let's say I observe two sequential events: P and then Q. If Q always follows right after P, then I might be observing cause-and-effect. But I could also be wrong."

"Why do I suspect there's another complicated word coming next?"

"A Latin phrase, actually: *post hoc ergo*

propter hoc. But we'll call it the ***post hoc* fallacy** for short. It means, 'after, therefore because of.' It's a misattribution of causality to sequential events. It's an easy mistake to make in the world of science when we observe one event follow after another. Like the proud rooster who thinks his crowing is what makes the sun rise every morning."

You begin to realize just how badly you could use a short nap to recharge your mental batteries.

Uncle notices your fatigue but is undaunted. "There's an old myth that says it will rain after you wash your car. But is there any scientific reason to suspect that the act of washing your car *causes* it to rain?"

"Common sense says no. But then why do such myths seem to persist?"

"I suspect it's a case of **confirmation bias**."

Egad. "You're going to explain, of course."

"Simple. It goes like this. Whenever we wash our car, we are more likely to notice when it rains afterward—an hour later, or a day later. In our minds, we associate the rain with washing the car. But there are many times we wash the car and it *doesn't* rain. And likewise, there are many times it rains but we haven't washed the car. Lots of data that if, examined carefully, would almost certainly show there is no correlation—and therefore no causality—but our mind filters out all the data except what supports our belief that *washing the car causes it to rain.*"

Only Uncle could call an explanation like that *simple*.

He takes notice of your consternation. "I'm ready for some afternoon coffee, and I can see that you're ready for a break."

As Uncle would say, *indeed*.

Chapter 12

As Uncle brews a fresh pot of coffee, you walk down to the mailbox to stretch your legs and clear your mind. The mailbox is empty, but it still serves the essential purpose of getting you out of the house for a few minutes. The afternoon is warm, and it appears that the gathering clouds might produce a shower here and there. You intentionally slow the pace back to the house in an effort to extend the break time—a literal slow walk.

"Ah," says Uncle as you step back into the house, "I was just getting ready to dispatch a search party." His point isn't missed. You might be dragging your feet.

Uncle hands you a fresh cup of coffee and takes the subtle cue to make the conversation a bit more engaging. "This morning we were discussing several different kinds of science. I mentioned that we'd come back to forensic science since it is the weakest. Are you ready to put on your *CSI* hat?" Uncle motions for the two of you to retake your seats in the living room.

As you ponder the question it occurs to you that the scientific method you've been discussing all day turns out to be pretty weak. How much weaker is forensic science going to be?

Uncle doesn't wait for an answer. "I'm also a fan of the show, so let me quote a good line for you. Supervisor Gil Grissom is in his office discussing a thorny case with Investigator Nick Stokes when he looks at Stokes and says something like, 'We need to reserve judgment until we get all the data.' What's wrong with Grissom's statement?

It takes a brief moment for your brain to

reengage. Yes, now you recall the scene Uncle is referring to. Grissom is a meticulous investigator and not prone to making mistakes. "I don't think I see it."

Uncle groans audibly. "This was supposed to be a softball question. You see, *scientists never have all the data.* And even if they *did* have all the data, they wouldn't know it. Remember from our previous discussion that scientists never know the extent of their own ignorance? Grissom might be missing that *one* critical piece of information that breaks the case in an unexpected direction. Just think about how often the plot of the show takes a dramatic turn as the result of some tiny scrap of seemingly insignificant forensic evidence, like a fleck of paint or a carpet fiber."

You nod slightly as the point sinks in.

Uncle continues. "Here's another way to

think about it. As the supervisor, Grissom likes to test his CSIs by walking through the scene of a crime and having them make a 'first take'—an initial impression of what happened based on the visible evidence. Always wrong, and almost pointless, except that it makes for good television drama."

Your mind is catching up again. "Because they're going to uncover more evidence that helps explain the crime."

"Yes. And as part of the audience, we may already know what happened. So we become the cheering section for our on-screen heroes as they try to unravel the crime." Uncle pauses. "Here's a simple analogy. Think of the crime like a jigsaw puzzle. You only have a few scattered pieces to work with, and the challenge is to figure out what the rest of the puzzle looks like."

"But the audience has already seen the

puzzle box top."

"So to speak. Now the CSIs have to find the puzzle pieces and put them together. A little like a treasure hunt."

You interject. "In the TV show, the usual procedure is to collect enough evidence to undermine the testimony of the prime suspect. To keep applying pressure until he confesses."

"Yes, which again takcs us back to our prior discussion. The suspect says one thing. 'I didn't do it. I have an alibi,' and so forth. But the forensic evidence says something else."

"Like an impartial witness. Somebody has to be wrong. So at some point, the suspect can't explain the evidence and is compelled to confess."

"Grissom wins again. Justice is served.

Tune in next week for the next thrilling episode."

"Okay, so if forensic evidence is so compelling when it comes to solving a crime, why do you say it's weak as a means of scientific discovery?"

Uncle is always pleased when you connect the dots and ask good questions. "Let's keep the discussion on *CSI* for a while longer in order to answer that question. Now tell me, as my CSI apprentice, which are the hardest crimes to solve?"

"Well, the crimes that have the least amount of evidence."

"Good start. Keep going."

"The CSIs say they like to have a 'fresh' crime scene that hasn't been contaminated."

"Yes! Follow the implications."

"The *older* the crime scene is, the harder it is to collect reliable evidence."

"Yes. Less evidence, more contamination, and the evidence you do collect could be quite degraded. The longer it's been since the crime occurred—generally speaking—the harder it will be for the CSIs to solve it."

"And the problem is compounded if it's an outdoor crime scene. Wind. Rain. Predation. That kind of stuff."

"Yes. The good evidence may be gone, and spurious evidence may take its place. Now remember what we're doing with forensic evidence. We're taking bits of data that are available for us to examine in the *present* and trying to piece together something that happened in the *past*."

"And the longer it's been since the event, the less evidence we have and the harder it is to piece it back together in order to solve the crime."

"You have the right idea."

"Okay . . . the longer it's been since the event, the more likely we are to be *wrong* about what really happened."

Ha! Uncle raises both arms in a mock victory salute.

Chapter 13

"When we run an experiment or make a direct observation, the data is literally right in front of us. In real time."

You connect the dots again. "It doesn't get any fresher. It would be like witnessing the crime as it happens. But the older the evidence, the more gaps it has. Fewer pieces of the puzzle, as you might say."

"The other thing to remember about forensic science is that we're trying to understand something we didn't see, *nor can it be repeated*. It's a one-time event. Most experiments, and many natural observations, can be repeated over and over. Repetition is part of what makes science more robust. That is, more certain of what it believes."

"But that doesn't apply to something like

the Big Bang. You can't repeat it in the laboratory."

"Correct. One-time events are highly problematical for science—and that's true *even when you observe them happen.* In fact, one-time events are practically worthless. Maybe you didn't see what you *thought* you saw. We know that eyewitness testimony is highly unreliable."

Uncle continues with an anecdote. "When I was in grad school, my advisor used to joke about publishing those interesting one-time observations in *The Journal of Irreproducible Results.* Kind of an inside joke. It would take an imaginary journal like that to publish your research, because no credible journal would publish results that couldn't be repeated."

"I'd never thought of that."

"Here's another silly question to illustrate

the difficulty of forensic science. *What color were the dinosaurs?* Think for a moment before you try to answer."

"Well. . . ."

"Careful. Think about the epistemological question—*'how do you know?'* What is your earliest recollection?"

"I want to say that I 'know' from picture books. The dinosaurs were all green. But then again . . . whoever colored the pictures has never seen a real dinosaur."

"Do you know what a T-Rex sounds like?"

"Only from a movie like *Jurassic Park*. But I'm pretty sure Steven Spielberg has never heard a T-Rex howl."

"Not even on the set. The sound effects were added in post production."

"So we have to fill in a lot of gaps . . . with our imagination."

"I prefer to call it speculation. But whatever you want to call it. . ."

"It isn't science."

Uncle nods. "Fossils don't come with labels that tell us what color they were or what kind of sound they made. Or even how long ago they were buried."

Uh oh. You sense that the conversation is about to take another turn. "But don't we know how old the fossil record is?"

"Do we?" Uncle likes to reflect your questions to see how you're thinking.

"Scientists say the dinosaurs became extinct 65 million years ago."

"I see. But if there are no dinosaur tombstones that say, 'Here Lies Our Beloved Bruno Brontosaurus. . . Born 65,000,050 B.C. . . . Died 65,000,000 B.C. in a Blaze of Glory. . . May He Forever Rest In Peace. . .' then what do we really have to go on?"

"We have to make some assumptions, don't we?"

"A few."

Chapter 14

Uncle leans back to continue. "Here's the way one popular young-earth creation scientist describes the situation: 'The debate is not about the *facts*. The debate is about the way we *interpret* the facts.' Not an exact quote, but that's to the best of my recollection. What do you suppose he's trying to say?"

"It sounds like he's saying that we all have the same facts in front of us—such as dinosaur bones—but that we don't all interpret facts in the same way."

"Think back to Gil Grissom's offhand remark to Nick Stokes. Now we could add that even if somehow we had all the facts, we'd still need a framework to interpret them."

You pick up the idea. "Facts alone are not

necessarily enough to piece together the past."

"And that's because there is often more than one way I could end up with a certain collection of facts. It would be like finding my fingerprints at a crime scene—say, a grocery store close to my home that was recently robbed by someone wearing a ski mask."

"Your fingerprints mean you've been in the store, but they don't necessarily mean you were in the store when it was robbed or that you had anything to do with the rob-bery."

"Which is why we have to be careful about making inferences from the facts. Now let's say we check the surveillance video, and six hours before the crime, I was in the store to buy my weekly supply of milk and eggs. Then we pull the register receipts to confirm the transaction. A gallon of whole milk and a dozen eggs, extra large."

"The more evidence we have, the clearer the picture becomes. Evidence provides additional context, which makes it possible to interpret the evidence more accurately."

"I suppose with enough evidence, we might agree there's only one way it all fits together. But it could be a different story when the evidence is thin. Now our *assumptions* can lead us to drastically different conclusions."

"For instance?"

"Let's say a young-earth creation scientist and an old-earth **uniformitarian** scientist are both digging for fossils in Montana."

"Sounds like you're about to tell a bad joke."

"I'm making up the story, but it's factually accurate. So our two scientists unearth a T-Rex thighbone. What does each one see? A bone? No, much more than a bone. The creation scientist sees the remains of an animal that was buried *alive* in a catastrophic flood and afterward was rapidly fossilized. The uniformitarian scientist sees an animal that was slowly buried *after* death and fossilized over millions of years."

"You can't get much further apart than that. But I don't think you defined 'uniformitarian.'"

"My apologies. *Uniformitarianism* a big word that refers to a belief that the slow geological processes we see in nature today—tectonics, erosion, sedimentation, and so forth—have been operational over long periods of time. Many, many millions of years. With the exception of some notable local catastrophes—volcanoes, hurricanes, earthquakes, tsunamis, and maybe a meteorite here and there—the general processes of nature are believed to be quite slow and therefore require long ages to produce what we see today."

"Processes like evolution?"

"Yes, evolution fits into the framework of long ages and gradual changes."

"But you'd argue that uniform. . ."

"*Uniformitarianism.*"

". . .that uniformitarianism is not a scientific theory."

"Test it for yourself and tell me."

"Well, you said it's based on the fact that we can observe the slow progress of geological processes today."

"True. No argument there. Go on."

"But the problem is we're having to make assumptions about what happened in the past—the distant past, before there was anyone to observe what was actually happening. Just because we observe slow processes over a few thousand years of human history, it might be dangerous to assume that it's been happening for *millions* of years."

"Or billions, for that matter. The old-earth scientist says that earth formed 4.5 *billion* years ago—just a few million years after the sun began to shine."

"If that's true, it's a really long time for us to guess what might have been going on."

"A few thousand years of direct observation would amount to nothing. Like a couple of moon rocks. And it would be separated in time from the beginning of the earth by 4.5 *billion* years."

"I'm afraid I still don't understand how you could end up with such diverging views of geology. It seems to me that we ought to have enough evidence to settle the question."

"Obviously not everyone would agree with that."

"But you?"

"I would put it this way. Uniformitarianism and long ages are popular ideas in part because there is some evidence that seems to fit the model in a compelling way. I wouldn't try to argue that it's entirely a matter of faith. But toss in some **anomalies** and things start to get more interesting."

"What do you mean by *anomalies*?"

"Something that doesn't fit the theory. Like the recent discovery of dinosaur remains that contain preserved soft tissue. The creation scientist says, 'Aha! Here's compelling proof of recent burial.' Meanwhile, the uniformitarian scientist says, 'Aha! Here's compelling proof that soft tissue can be preserved for millions of years.'"

"Facts don't necessarily settle the argument."

"They do not. Now, to be honest, I used to believe in an old universe before I became a Christian. The size and apparent age of the universe are facts that we have to acknowledge. And even now I can't explain how or why God created the universe in a way that makes it look so big and so old."

"Uncle, that really surprises me. I thought you were a young-earth guy from start to finish."

"Hardly. But as I have grown in my understanding of Christian doctrine—and especially **apologetics**—I'm in a better position to observe how our beliefs about the age of the universe are shaped most drastically by our starting assumptions."

"I'm not sure I know what you mean by *apologetics*."

"It simply refers to a systematic defense of biblical truth. In many ways, it's what we've been doing in these long conversations—examining truth claims and the underlying assumptions we use to build a worldview. The most important assumption that separates the young-earth creationist and the old-earth uniformitarian is the question of God's existence. We start with drastically different assumptions, and we consequently come to drastically different interpretations of the facts."

"Are you sure about that? Because I thought there were quite a number of people who believe in God *and* an old universe—you know, that God used long ages to form the earth and used evolution to create life."

"You are correct that many try to claim both biblical theism and an old universe.

There are even a handful of theories that attempt to reconcile 'six day creation' with the ideas of evolution and long ages. But when we look carefully at the issue from the vantage point of the Christian worldview—without the biases inherent to atheistic science—we see that the only view consistent with the whole teaching of the Bible is a young universe."

You hesitate for a moment. "Can I ask you a personal question?"

"You may."

"Does your belief in six-day creation make you uncomfortable? I mean, do you have any doubts about it? As you pointed out, the scientific evidence for an old universe looks compelling."

"It's a fair question. I'm comfortable defending six-day creation. Besides, I could answer in part by pointing out that just within the last few generations the scientific explanation for the origin of the universe has changed drastically—and I would argue, it's changed for the worse. Do you remember us talking about the test of scientific progress?"

"Theories are always changing." And then you quickly add, "Because our knowledge is always expanding. But what do you mean about the theory of origins changing for the *worse*?"

"Simply that our current scientific consensus—the Big Bang theory, which as you know by now, isn't a theory at all—requires us to believe, as an article of faith, that the universe created itself out of nothing. But before we latched onto the Big Bang, we were inclined to believe that the universe was eternal."

"And how is that a better explanation?"

"Because it acknowledges the philosophical implications of causality. Namely, that for anything at all to exist, *something* in the universe must be eternal. The Big Bang is flatly irrational, because nothing can create itself."

"So there is nothing irrational about the existence of an eternal *Creator*?"

"Like it or not, God's existence is a rational necessity."

Chapter 15

You're pretty sure you agree with Uncle's conclusion, but something is still bothering you. "Don't scientists tell us that belief in God is *unscientific*?"

Uncle laughs. "Of course. It all comes back to your starting assumptions. The atheist starts with the assumption that God *doesn't* exist, then he goes looking for a way to explain how we got here without God."

"Evolution."

"And an old universe, because evolution is a very slow, inefficient process of change and so-called progress. It requires lots and lots of time to have any credibility."

"But it isn't necessary in a creation framework."

"No, not *necessary*. If God is God, he can

create in any way that pleases him and serves his purposes. Fast or slow, orderly or chaotic. Now, the Bible says, without ambiguity, that God finished the work of creation in six regular days—'morning and evening were the *first* day,' and the *second* day, and so on. And that it was a very orderly and purposeful process of giving form to the universe and bringing life into it."

You give Uncle a puzzled expression.

"You want me to explain it in scientific terms? It can't be done. No matter what you choose to believe, creation cannot be explained in terms of what we would call 'natural laws.' Neither can we explain the origin of life. It requires a miracle no matter how you slice it."

Chapter 16

The sun is now beginning to fade, and to your surprise, the afternoon has passed without any rain showers. If the intense conversation with Uncle Bob is going to continue for much longer, you'll need a break along with something to eat. Uncle senses a lull in the discussion. "I don't want to wear out my welcome—or my nephew. But if you want to take a dinner break, maybe we can finish up before dark."

"I'm definitely ready for a break and a bite to eat."

"Remember, it's my turn to buy."

Thirty minutes later the pizza is delivered and you're back at the kitchen table to eat. Uncle smothers his pizza with Parmesan cheese and then picks up the discussion without a preamble. "Let's close the loop. Something you read recently was really bothering you—which prompted today's long discussion about science. Have we covered the issues that were on your mind?"

Uncle reaches for another slice of pizza while you think through the day. If anything, this discussion was even more intense than the last one, and you're struggling to assimilate it.

You finally find the words to express your feelings. "It really bothers me that so many people try to portray science as this singular voice of reason when it simply can't be the case."

Uncle puts clearer words to your exasperation. "You wonder just how many of the things scientists say are overly confident assertions designed to mask the persistent doubts they have about their own beliefs."

At moments like this you realize Uncle is three steps ahead of you and waiting patiently for you to catch up. He continues.

"Within the world of science there always is—and always *must* be—vigorous disagreement. Otherwise we can never learn anything. Science can't progress if it becomes overly dogmatic—too in love with its own ideas. The nature of science is chaotic and unpredictable. Often ambiguous and confrontational. Always skeptical."

"But that hardly seems to come out in the media. Instead you get just one side of what must be an extremely complex issue, and the attitude is often dismissive toward anyone who disagrees."

Uncle interjects. "You're referring to the so-called 'consensus' of scientific opinion?"

"Yes. And it's interesting that you said it that way."

"I try to choose my words carefully. Scientific theories are just guesses. That's all they can ever be. As we've seen today, we can never claim that our theories are *proven*. They must be treated loosely—because the odds are they'll change soon. A dedicated scientist should be the most skeptical. And he should be most skeptical about the beliefs he claims to be the most certain of. He ought to know this will be his blind spot."

"So what then does a 'consensus' prove, if anything?"

"That's a question that would take a while to unpack. But let me try to offer an over-simplified explanation. Scientifically, a consensus of opinion *proves* nothing. You might recall in our last discussion that I quoted a Christian teacher who pointed out that 'Opinions have no argumentative weight.' Which means by logical extension that no *consensus* of opinion has any argumentative weight, either. Any clever fellow can build a consensus about anything by carefully selecting the sample and asking the right question. Opinion surveys are notoriously biased."

"But shouldn't the opinion of *scientists* count more than the average Joe's?"

Uncle laughs. "Not necessarily. You've stumbled onto something called the **expert fallacy**. It's the belief that an expert's opinion has more weight than the average Joe's. Very dangerous."

"Why is that?"

"I'd like you to try to answer that question yourself."

You pause to reflect a moment while Uncle polishes off another slice of pizza. "I suppose it's dangerous because the average Joe is inclined to go along with the opinion of the expert. Joe *assumes* the expert is in a better position to know what's true. And that might not be the case."

"Well said, *very* well said. Experts are wrong all the time about the very things they are supposed to be the experts in. Now, I know you find my use of terminology to be tedious, but here's another idea for you to digest. It's called **information cascade** and it means—in simple terms—that Joe believes what the expert says because the expert believes it first. For many things it's just easier to pick up someone else's beliefs rather than taking time to examine every belief for ourselves."

"So information cascade is like a mental shortcut?"

"Good way to put it. Now, as for the formation of a consensus, it helps to remember that most people are pack animals. Group identity—and group approval—is extremely important to us, personally and professionally. Only a few stalwarts are 'mavericks' or 'Lone Rangers' who are comfortable operating independently. It's rather natural for people to develop a general consensus of opinion around a certain idea, regardless of how weak or strong the evidence is. That's why we need mavericks to point out the flaws in the consensus. To swim against the tide, as the expression goes. And that takes a lot of courage."

"So we shouldn't ignore dissenting voices just because they're part of a small minority."

"The history of science shows that progress often comes from the maverick who doesn't allow himself to be constrained by the established rules and beliefs of the consensus."

"Like Einstein?"

"Good example. He was an outsider to the world of physics when he proposed the theory of relativity."

"So why is it that those who are part of the consensus seem to despise the maverick?"

"Another short answer to a long question. It's because the consensus develops considerable influence, and any dissenting idea represents a threat to the established power structure."

You're completely taken aback by Uncle's comment. After a moment to recover, you say, "If that's really the case, then consensus has more to do with *control* than it has to do with *truth*."

"You said it. Scientists are not exempt from the fallen human tendency to accumulate power to themselves and then to project that power over others. That means, first of all, keeping the troops in line—maintaining conformity *within* the group—and secondly, exerting the collective influence of the group on those who are *outside* of it. Sometimes using proxies—like politicians or judges—to accomplish the latter goal."

Once again you're stunned by what Uncle just said. "Whatever happened to scientific objectivity?"

Uncle looks at you across the table while you ponder the answer to your own question.

Chapter 17

After a few long minutes of silence, Uncle changes gears abruptly. It's time to bring the conversation to a conclusion. "The pizza was excellent, and I have immensely enjoyed our time together again today."

Without waiting for a response, Uncle pushes back from the table and begins to clear the plates and leftovers. "I know you have a great deal to think about, and you'll have many more questions. I am already looking forward to our next conversation."

Uncle quietly makes his way to the front door. As he slips into the darkening night you hear him say, "Thanks again for the coffee!" The door closes behind him with a soft click and the house is silent except for the ticking of the kitchen clock.

You remain frozen at the table, hardly able to move until you notice your foot starting to fall asleep. As you begin to get up from the table, you realize you'll never be able to see science the same way again.

Review Questions

You may find the following questions helpful to review key ideas in the book and/or use this book for group study and discussion.

1. Think of a recent example of a scientific study you heard about in the news. What were some notable questions or issues the report failed to address?
2. How does science end up mixing faith with its facts?
3. What are the primary ways that science discovers new knowledge? What are the strengths and weaknesses of each?
4. Why must we assume that scientific theories are true until disproved by the evidence? How is this similar to the

courtroom situation?

5. What are the two types of decision-making errors and why is it impossible to eliminate them?

6. What do we mean when we say that induction makes it possible to make inferences?

7. In what sense are scientific theories—*models*—useful? In what sense are they always intentionally wrong?

8. How do the axioms of induction, uniformity, and the reliability of sense perception have to work together to make scientific inquiry possible?

9. How do biases affect our expectations and add to the resistance we have to exploring new ideas?

10. How does confirmation bias lead us into the trap of the *post hoc* fallacy?

11. What does forensic science attempt to do

and why is it more likely to draw wrong conclusions?

12. What does the example of the dinosaurs teach us in regard to the limitations of forensic science?

13. How do our prior assumptions shape our interpretation of facts to such an extent that diverging conclusions are possible?

14. How is the theory of evolution used to 'prove' that God doesn't exist? What makes this a weak argument?

15. What role do anomalies play in the progress of science?

16. What are the dangers of following a consensus of opinion? Why are we prone to accept the consensus as truth?

Glossary

anomalies—unusual observations that do not fit the prevailing hypothesis; anomalies often point to the inadequacies of the current belief.

apologetics—a systematic defense of Christian truth.

axiom—a principle that must be assumed because it cannot be proved; axioms are the building blocks for knowledge.

burden of proof—the evidence that is required to shift a conclusion away from its default position.

causality—the law that every effect must have an antecedent cause.

confirmation bias—the tendency to notice data that agrees with one's preconceived ideas and to ignore data that disagrees.

consensus—a general agreement of opinion regarding the reliability of a scientific hypothesis.

correlation (correlated)—an apparent relationship between two or more observable characteristics; correlation alone is not enough to establish causality.

epistemology—the science of knowledge.

experiment (experimental science)—collecting data by manipulating a natural system in a way that makes it possible to study the effects of changing the system's inputs.

expert fallacy—the assumption that a statement is true because of the expertise of the person making the claim.

fallacy of consensus—the assumption that a statement must be true because most people believe it.

forensics (forensic science)—using evidence

available in the present to make inferences about events that took place in the past.

groupthink—the tendency for the members of a certain group to reinforce each others' common belief.

hypothesis—an assumption about the nature of reality that is usually based on theory and/or observation and is useful for pursuing further investigation. The hypothesis is customarily assumed to be true until proven false.

induction—the extrapolation from specific examples to general principles; this makes it possible to draw general conclusions from small amounts of data.

information cascade—the transmission of an idea or action from one person to another.

model—an approximation of a physical system; models help explain past behavior and can be used to predict future behavior.

observation (observational science)—collecting data from a natural system without interfering with its operation.

post hoc fallacy (*post hoc ergo propter hoc*)—after, therefore because of; the mistaken attribution of cause-and-effect to events that occur in sequence.

prediction—the ability to forecast future events before they occur.

presumption of guilt—beginning with the assumption of guilt; the burden of proof is on the accused to prove innocence.

presumption of innocence—beginning with the assumption of innocence; the burden of proof is on the accuser to prove guilt.

presuppositions—assumptions that come first and serve as the building blocks of knowledge.

relativity (Einstein's theory)—as used in this book, relativity is the hypothesis that gravitational attraction is the result of space-time warped by the mass of celestial bodies; more generally, relativity is the interdependence of matter, time, and space.

sampling (random, nonrandom)—collecting a subset of data from a population; the sample is said to be random if all the members of the population have an equal chance of being selected. In practice, most samples are biased in one way or another.

sense perception—the ability to gain objective knowledge by means of one's senses (sight, sound, smell, taste, touch).

theory (theoretical science)—an explanation of reality derived from underlying principles of science.

<u>Type 1 Error</u> (missed defect)—the decision-making error that occurs when we wrongly classify a bad item as good; Type 1 Errors increase as we try to eliminate Type 2 Errors.

<u>Type 2 Error</u> (false call)—the decision-making error that occurs when we wrongly classify a good item as bad; Type 2 Errors increase as we try to eliminate Type 1 Errors.

<u>uniformitarian</u> (uniformitarianism)—the belief that gradual geological processes acting in the present have been in effect over long ages, leading to the geological formations we see today.

<u>uniformity</u>—a belief in the constancy of physical relationships across time and space; uniformity makes it possible to observe effects today and to use that

knowledge to predict the same effects to-morrow.

Acknowledgements

Many thanks to my readers and reviewers for your helpful suggestions.

Acknowledgements

About the Author

J.R. Dickens completed a Ph.D. in mechanical engineering and enjoys writing and speaking on topics like philosophy, ethics, and Christian apologetics. He can be reached by email at jrdickens90@gmail.com.